# AMERICA'S CHILDREN

*Real-Life Stories and Poems*
*About Children, Past and Present*

Selected by LINDA ETKIN *and* BEBE WILLOUGHBY

## A GOLDEN BOOK • NEW YORK

Western Publishing Company, Inc., Racine, Wisconsin 53404

Library of Congress Catalog Card Number: 92-71616 ISBN: 0-307-15876-4/
ISBN: 0-307-65876-7 (lib. bdg.)      MCMXCII

# ACKNOWLEDGMENTS

The editor and publisher have made every effort to trace the ownership of all copyrighted material and to secure permission from copyright holders. Any errors or omissions are inadvertent, and the publisher will be pleased to make the necessary corrections in future printings. Thanks to the following authors, publishers, and agents for permission to use the material indicated:

Tony Augustyniak for "Old Woman and Robots." Reprinted by permission on behalf of the author. All rights reserved.

Estelle Barlow for "Playhouse Memories" from *Growing Up in the Depression*. Copyright © 1978 by Vantage Press. Reprinted by permission of the author. All rights reserved.

Susan Bergholz Literary Services for "Chanclas" from *The House on Mango Street* by Sandra Cisneros. Copyright © 1984, 1991 by Sandra Cisneros. Published by Vintage Books, a division of Random House, Inc., New York. Originally published in somewhat different form by Arte Publico Press in 1984 and revised in 1989.

Brandt & Brandt Literary Agents, Inc., for "Peregrine White and Virginia Dare" from *A Book of Americans* by Rosemary and Stephen Vincent Benét. Copyright © 1933. Copyright renewed 1961 by Rosemary Carr Benét. Reprinted by permission of Brandt & Brandt Literary Agents, Inc.

Nathan Breckenridge for "Dear Oscar." Reprinted by permission on behalf of the author. All rights reserved.

John Bridges for "Crew Cut" from "Shear Energy." Reprinted by permission of the author. All rights reserved.

Children's Television Workshop for "Dear Sesame Street." Sesame Street and the Sesame Street sign are trademarks and service marks of Children's Television Workshop. Sesame Street Muppet characters © 1992 Jim Henson Productions, Inc. Reprinted by permission of Children's Television Workshop. All rights reserved.

Cobblestone Publishing, Inc., for "The Story My Grandmother Told Me," an excerpt from "The Story My Grandmother Told Me" by Cornelia Arvanti Erskine; Cobblestone's Apr. issue: © 1981. "Growing Up in World War II" by Priscilla M. Harding; Cobblestone's Dec. issue: © 1985. "Annie Oakely: Sharpshooter," an excerpt from "Train Ride to Her Future" by Ellen Levine; Cobblestone's Jan. issue: © 1991. Reprinted by permission of Cobblestone Publishing, Inc., Peterborough, NH.

The Walt Disney Company for permission to illustrate Mickey Mouse, pages 56 and 69, and Mouseketeer cap, page 67. Copyright © 1992 The Walt Disney Company. All rights reserved.

Doubleday for "The Little Orphan Annie Secret Decoder Pin" from *In God We Trust, All Others Pay Cash* by Jean Shepherd. Copyright © 1966 by Jean Shepherd. Published by Doubleday, a division of Bantam Doubleday Dell, Inc.

Free To Be Foundation, Inc., for "Free to Be . . . You and Me," an excerpt from *Free to Be . . . You and Me* entitled "When We Grow Up." Music by Stephen Lawrence and lyrics by Shelley Miller. Copyright © 1972 Ms. Foundation for Women, Inc. Used by permission.

Mrs. Alfred Freidrich for "My Trip to the World's Fair, 1939" by Anna Litowinska. Reprinted by permission of Mrs. Alfred Freidrich. All rights reserved.

HarperCollins Publishers for "Cattle in the Hay," text only, from *On the Banks of Plum Creek* by Laura Ingalls Wilder; illustrated by Garth Williams. Text copyright 1937 by Laura Ingalls Wilder. Copyright © renewed 1963 by Roger L. McBride. Pictures copyright 1953 by Garth Williams. Copyright © renewed 1981 by Garth Williams. "We Chased Butterflies" from *Plenty Coups, Chief of the Crows* by Frank B. Linderman. Copyright © 1930 by Frank B. Linderman. Copyright renewed by Norma Linderman Waller, Verne Linderman, and Wilda Linderman. Reprinted by permission of HarperCollins Publishers.

Highlights for Children, Inc., for "Harriet Tubman" by Seth Uselman. Copyright © 1991. Used by permission of Highlights for Children, Inc., Columbus, OH.

Meg and Jeff Lindaman for "Conservation Rap." Reprinted with permission on behalf of the authors. All rights reserved.

Chelsea Mooser for "From Day to Night and Back Again." Reprinted with permission on behalf of the author. All rights reserved.

William Morrow & Company, Inc., for "Specs Toporcer," a text excerpt from pp. 259, 261, and 262 of *The Glory of Their Times* by Lawrence S. Ritter. New preface and chapters 5, 2, and 25 copyright © 1984 by Lawrence S. Ritter. Remainder copyright © 1966 by Lawrence S. Ritter. Reprinted by permission of William Morrow & Company, Inc. "On King Island," a text excerpt from pp. 29, 31, and 32 from *Good-bye My Island* by Jean Rogers. Copyright © 1983 by Jean Rogers. Reprinted by permission of Greenwillow Books, a division of William Morrow & Company, Inc.

Natural Resources Defense Council for "We Love the Earth." Reprinted by permission of NRDC. All rights reserved.

Oak Tree Publications, Inc., for "The Street" from *Horsecars and Cobblestones* by Sophie Ruskay. Copyright © 1958 A. S. Barnes. Reprinted by permission of Oak Tree Publications.

Penguin Books USA, Inc., for "Chano's First Buffalo Hunt" from *Tonweya and the Eagles* by Rosebud Yellow Robe. Copyright © 1979 by Rosebud Yellow Robe Frantz. Used by permission of Dial Books for Young Readers, a division of Penguin Books USA, Inc.

Random House, Inc., for "Elizabeth Eckford Tries to Go to School" from *The Long Shadow of Little Rock* by Daisy Bates. Copyright © 1962 David McKay. "The War Ended on Liberty Street" from *We Shook the Family Tree* by Hildegarde Dolson. Copyright © 1941, 1942, 1946, and renewed 1970 by Hildegarde Dolson. Reprinted by permission of Random House, Inc.

Danièle Rottkamp for "Humpty Dumpty." Reprinted with permission on behalf of the author. All rights reserved.

Katie Shearer for "Dear Prairie Dawn." Reprinted with permission on behalf of the author. All rights reserved.

Teachers and Writers Collaborative for "Peaceville" by John Reynolds, "Disco Dancing" by Richard Soto, and "Never Take Drugs," a Class Collaboration—I.S. 10, New York City, from *It's Not My Time for the Blues*, copyright © 1979. Reprinted by permission of Teachers and Writers Collaborative, 5 Union Square West, New York, NY 10003.

Tribune Media Services for permission to illustrate Annie, pages 56 and 63. © & ® Tribune Media Services. All rights reserved.

Helaina and Andrew Tuchfeld for "Dear Sesame Characters." Reprinted with permission on behalf of the authors. All rights reserved.

Omar Usmani for "Jack and Jill." Reprinted with permission on behalf of the author. All rights reserved.

**All of the artwork for this book has been specially commissioned from the following artists:**

*Joe Ewers:* Pages 76-77, 82-83, 89
*Michael Furuya:* Pages 37, 51, 85, 90-91, 92
*John Gampert:* Pages 7-9, 16, 40, 55-56, 67, 75, 81, 93
*Donald Gates:* Pages 60-61, 63
*Konrad Hack:* Pages 39, 47-49, 57, 65-66
*Ron Himler:* Pages 12-13, 23, 28-36
*Darcy May:* Pages 20-21, 78-79
*Diane Paterson:* Cover
*Gail Piazza:* Pages 72, 87, 88
*James Ransome:* Pages 11, 15, 25-27
*Mary Beth Schwark:* Pages 69-71
*Barbara Steadman:* Pages 52-53, 84

**Photos reprinted with permission of the following:**

*The Bettmann Archive:* Page 80
*Brown Brothers:* Pages 41(top), 43 (top), 58
*Culver Pictures:* Pages 42 (bottom), 43 (top), 59
*National Park Service, Ellis Island Immigration Museum:* Page 41 (bottom)
*New York Public Library:* Page 42 (top and middle)
*H. Armstrong Roberts:* Page 74

# CONTENTS

# INTRODUCTION

This is a book for children, about children. The stories, poems, and letters presented here describe growing up in America.

The "basics" of growing up—games to play, lessons to learn, friendships, and family ties—never seem to change at all. Yet each generation enjoys its own favorite games, toys, books, songs, and styles. And each meets the unique challenges of its time. Children in the 1800s settled with their families on the Western frontier, while at the turn of the century, children immigrated to this country from distant lands. Children of the 1940s grew up in a country at war, while children of the 1960s and 1970s faced sweeping social changes.

Many of the selections in this book were written by children who tell about the time in which they lived from their own special perspective. But all of the writers, young and old, can help us see how, as Americans, we have brought together many different cultures to create one community and one history.

Most of all, this is a book to enjoy and to help us imagine what it was like to grow up in America twenty—or even two hundred and twenty—years ago.

# In Colonial Days . . .

The *Mayflower* arrived at Plymouth, Massachusetts, on December 26, 1620. Thirty-five Pilgrims were aboard, including two babies born at sea.

Favorite children's games were hide-and-seek, hopscotch, blindman's buff, lawn bowling, ball games (like cricket), and singing games.

Favorite toys were hoops, rocking horses, kites, marbles, and dolls made of wood, corn husks, china, or rags.

Children were usually educated at home. Boys were taught to read and write using a Bible and hornbooks, which were wooden paddles with letters and numbers painted on them. Girls were taught music, sewing, dancing, and drawing.

The first public school in the colonies opened in Massachusetts in 1629.

Thanksgiving was first celebrated in 1621 after the Pilgrims' first harvest. The Pilgrims and Indians shared a feast of turkey, popcorn, maple candy, and other foods.

# PEREGRINE WHITE AND VIRGINIA DARE

*Peregrine White and Virginia Dare were both born in
early settlements of the New World. Virginia Dare was
the first baby born on Roanoke Island in the Virginia
Colony in 1587. Peregrine White was born on the*
Mayflower *in 1620. They were among the first of
America's children.*

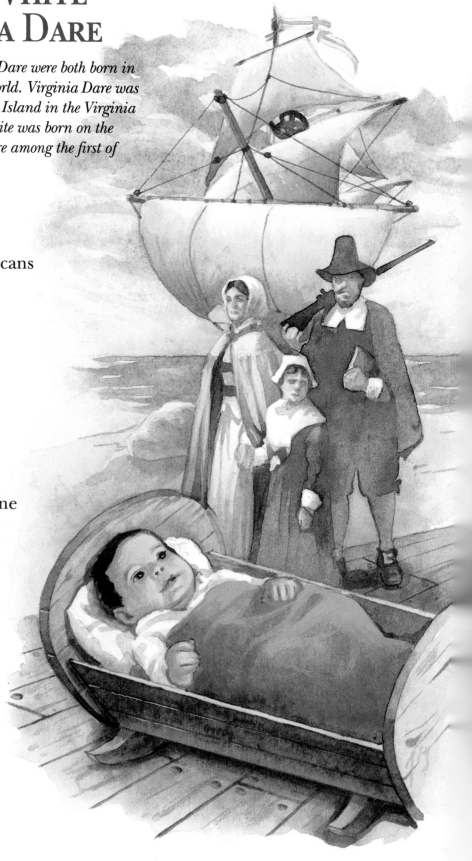

Peregrine White
And Virginia Dare
Were the first real Americans
Anywhere.

Others might find it
Strange to come
Over the ocean
To make a home.

England and memory
Left behind—
But Virginia and Peregrine
Didn't mind.

One of them born
On Roanoke,
And the other cradled
In Pilgrim oak.

Rogues might bicker
And good men pray.
Did they pay attention?
No, not they.

Men might grumble
And women weep
But Virginia and Peregrine
Went to sleep.

They had their dinner
And napped and then
When they woke up
It was dinner again.

They didn't worry,
They didn't wish,
They didn't farm
And they didn't fish.

There was lots of work
But they didn't do it.
They were pioneers
But they never knew it.

Wolves in the forest
And Indian drums!
Virginia and Peregrine
Sucked their thumbs.

They were only babies.
They didn't care.
Peregrine White
And Virginia Dare.

*Rosemary and
Stephen Vincent Benét*

# A Letter From the New World

*America's earliest settlers had to endure New England winters, which were long and very cold. This colonial child, Judith March, was allowed to bring her dog to church for warmth. But she never expected her pet to join the choir!*

Dear Anna,

I was eleven years old yesterday. It was the Sabbath, and I did the wickedest thing I ever did in all my life. I laughed right out in meeting. It was dreadful. The minister stopped and looked straight at me, everybody looked at me, and I was so ashamed. Father gazed up at the gallery as if he did not know anything had happened; and I could feel how shamed Mother was. Oh, I was never so wicked before.

This is what made me laugh. The people were singing:

> *"With reverence let the saints appear*
> *And bow before the Lord,"*

and they sang it:

> *"And  bow-ow-ow, and  bow-ow-ow."*

The meetinghouse is so cold that Mother has a sheepskin bag nailed to the seat to keep her feet warm, and Father lets me bring Ponto. He lies down in front of me and I put my feet on his back. He is the best dog in the meeting; but this time, almost before the people had stopped singing, "And bow-ow-ow," he called out, "Bow-wow-wow" in that big grum voice of his. I suppose he had a bad dream. That was when I laughed.

Mother never punishes any of us on the Sabbath, but the first thing Monday morning she told me how bad I had been. She said I must spend the day so I should remember it. Then she put a chair with the back to the window and gave me my knitting and said I must knit all day.

*Written by Judith March of Newbury, Massachusetts, to her cousin, Anna Maitland, in England, on February 21, 1664*

*Adapted from* Letters From Colonial Children *by Eva March Tappan*

# A Printer's Devil

*Benjamin Franklin is remembered as an inventor and a patriot who helped write the Declaration of Independence. But even Ben Franklin had to go to school and learn the trade his father chose for him, much like any other boy of his time. An apprentice in a printer's shop, like Franklin, was called a "printer's devil."*

Josiah, my father, married young, and brought his wife with three children into New England, about 1682. By the same wife he had four more children born there, and by a second wife ten more, in all seventeen. I was the youngest son and born in Boston, New England.

I was put in grammar school at the age of eight. I had already learned how to read at a very early age. (In fact, I do not remember when I could not read.) But after not quite one year my father took me from the grammar school, and sent me to a school for writing and arithmetic.

At ten years old I was taken home to assist my father in his business, which was that of a tallow chandler and soap-boiler. I was put to work cutting wick for the candles, filling the dipping mold and the molds for cast candles, attending the shop, going on errands, etc.

I disliked the work and dreamed of becoming a sailor, but my father would not permit it. However, living near the water, I was much in and about the sea. I learned early to swim well, and to manage boats. I was generally a leader among the boys I knew, and sometimes led them into scrapes.

I continued in my father's business for two years, that is, till I was twelve years old.

From a child I was fond of reading, and the little bit of money that came into my hands was used to buy books. This bookish inclination finally determined my father to make me a printer. He already had one son (James) of that profession.

In 1717, my brother James returned from England with a press and letters to set up his business in Boston. I liked the printer's trade much better than that of my father, but still had a hankering for the sea. To prevent this, my father was impatient to have me bound to my brother as an apprentice in his shop.

I put it off for some time, but at last was persuaded. I signed the papers when I was yet but twelve years old. I was to serve as an apprentice till I was twenty-one years of age. In a little time I made great progress in the business and became a useful hand to my brother.

I now had access to better books. I became friendly with the apprentices of booksellers and they sometimes let me borrow a small book, which I was careful to return soon and clean. Often I sat up in my room reading for almost the entire night, when the book was borrowed in the evening and to be returned early in the morning, lest it should be missed or wanted.

*Adapted from Benjamin Franklin's* Autobiography

# ELIZABETH ZANE:
## A Heroine of the American Revolution

*Stories of Revolutionary War heroes, such as George Washington and Patrick Henry, are certainly well known. But many women and even children played a part in winning America's independence. Their stories are less widely known, but their deeds were no less heroic.*

Elizabeth Zane was only fifteen when the American colonies began their fight for independence from British rule in 1775. She lived with her family near the Wheeling River and Fort Henry in the Virginia Colony. The fort was an important outpost for the colonists and a likely target for the British.

In October 1777, a British soldier named Simon Girty gathered a group of five hundred Indians and led an attack upon the fort. The soldiers, their families, and all who lived nearby quickly fled behind the fort's high wooden walls for protection. There were only twelve soldiers to defend the colonists, and they fired back as fast as they could reload their guns.

Suddenly the soldiers realized that their gunpowder was almost gone. The nearest supply was at a house nearly two hundred feet from the fort's huge gates. Many of the soldiers volunteered to go. Then Elizabeth Zane stepped forward. She pleaded with them to let her go. The idea of sending a young girl on such a dangerous task was unthinkable to the soldiers. But she insisted, saying that every man who could handle a gun was needed at the fort. Finally Elizabeth was allowed to go.

The gates of Fort Henry slowly swung open. Elizabeth's heart beat wildly as she stepped out and quickly walked toward the house. Amazingly, the enemy did not fire at her. Maybe they took pity on her because she was so young. Elizabeth ran inside the house, found the small keg of gunpowder, and wrapped it in a tablecloth. Then she tied the bundle around her waist. Taking a deep breath, she stepped outside again and ran toward the fort's gates as fast as she could.

By now the enemy had guessed her mission. They fired a shower of arrows and bullets at her. But somehow Elizabeth reached the fort unharmed. Safely inside again, she was surrounded by the cheering soldiers and her friends and family. The small but precious keg of gunpowder actually saved the colonists, for it allowed the soldiers to defend the fort long enough for help to arrive.

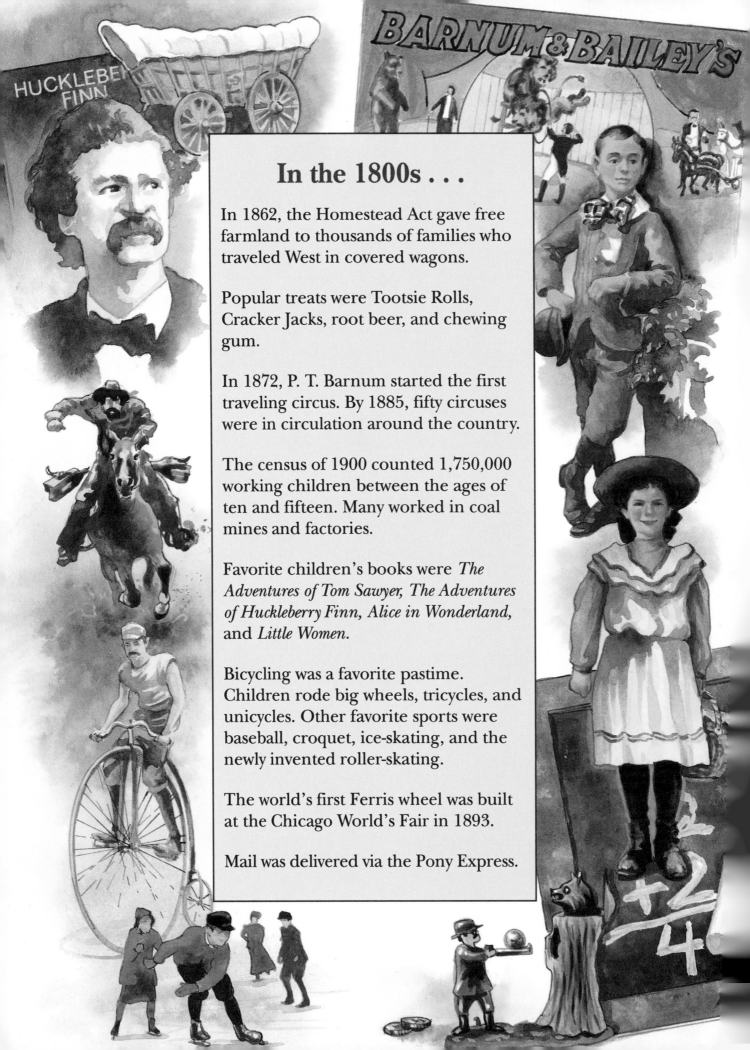

# In the 1800s . . .

In 1862, the Homestead Act gave free farmland to thousands of families who traveled West in covered wagons.

Popular treats were Tootsie Rolls, Cracker Jacks, root beer, and chewing gum.

In 1872, P. T. Barnum started the first traveling circus. By 1885, fifty circuses were in circulation around the country.

The census of 1900 counted 1,750,000 working children between the ages of ten and fifteen. Many worked in coal mines and factories.

Favorite children's books were *The Adventures of Tom Sawyer, The Adventures of Huckleberry Finn, Alice in Wonderland,* and *Little Women.*

Bicycling was a favorite pastime. Children rode big wheels, tricycles, and unicycles. Other favorite sports were baseball, croquet, ice-skating, and the newly invented roller-skating.

The world's first Ferris wheel was built at the Chicago World's Fair in 1893.

Mail was delivered via the Pony Express.

# ANNIE OAKLEY:
## *Sharpshooter*

*Annie Oakley first learned how to hunt to help her family. She never dreamed that one day these same skills would make her a worldwide star in the Wild West Shows.*

It all started on a Friday the 13th in 1860, when Annie was born Phoebe Ann Moses. Right from the beginning, everyone called her Annie. She grew up in a small log cabin with her mother, father, five sisters, and brother.

Farm life on the Ohio frontier was hard, but Annie loved being outdoors. She roamed the woods, gathering nuts and berries and learning the habits of wild animals.

One bitter winter night, Annie's father was caught in a blizzard as he returned from a trip to the grain mill. Jacob lay ill and feverish for a long time and then died. Susan Moses was left to raise seven children alone.

Although Annie was not quite seven, she wanted to help her struggling family. But how? As she sat playing with cornstalks and string one day, she figured out how to make small traps for quail. Then she waited—and waited. Success! For the first time in weeks, the Moses family had meat for dinner.

There are many stories about how Annie first learned to handle a gun. Most likely it happened this way:

One morning Annie's mother was off on a nursing trip, and Annie and her brother, John, were alone at home. The old family rifle hung above the fireplace, rusty and unused since their father's death. Annie felt challenged, as well as hungry for the taste of meat other than quail.

With John's help, she got the rifle down. Then out to the fields they went. Resting the heavy rifle on a fence post, she took aim at a squirrel. Bang! The rifle kicked back with a powerful force, bruising her face. Years later, Annie would smile and point to a small scar on her chin or nose and say that the mark was the result of her first attempt to use a gun.

Annie's mother married again and had another baby girl, but the family situation became desperate. One day a man drove up to the home and asked if there was a young girl who could come to live with him and his wife and care for their newborn baby. He said he would pay a salary of fifty cents a week and send the child to school.

Annie's mother gave her permission to take the job, and off she went to her new home. She was excited about having a chance to

learn to read *and* get paid for her work.

But the man had deceived her, and Annie's two-year stint with the family became a nightmare. Each day she was forced to work from early morning to past midnight. Sometimes she was beaten, and she was never shown any warmth or kindness. She was never told that her stepfather had died and that her mother had written begging that she be sent home.

Annie had such a terrible experience that she vowed never to speak the name of the family. To this day, no one knows for certain who they were. Annie simply called them "the wolves."

One day when the wolves were away on a trip, Annie planned her escape. She finished her chores so that when they returned, they would not immediately know she had run away. Then she walked hurriedly to the train station and boarded the first train headed for Greenville. She told her story to an elderly man sitting next to her. When the conductor approached and heard the story, he gave her a free pass for the trip.

Once home, Annie learned that her mother had remarried again. Annie liked her new stepfather, whom everyone called Grandpap Shaw. But the family was still very poor, and Annie took to the woods and fields to find food. She practiced shooting until she became one of the most skilled sharpshooters in the county.

Annie was never one to take the easy shot at a sitting bird or other animal. She did not think it gave the animal a fair chance, she said. So when she spotted game, she would flush it out, twirl around, sometimes do a somersault, and then take aim. She was such a good shot that the men and boys who went to the turkey shoots refused to let her enter the contests. She began selling much of the game she shot to a storekeeper in nearby Greenville.

Before she was fourteen, Annie had earned enough money selling her game to pay off what was owed on the family home. Annie's game birds were so cleanly shot through the head that they were shipped from Greenville to be served in restaurants in the best hotels in Cincinnati. And now Annie herself was on her way to the big city.

*From "Train Ride to Her Future"*
*by Ellen Levine*

# MARY'S LAMB

*Today, it is hard to imagine a school that is only one big room. But long ago, children of all different ages were taught together by one teacher. This story is about a certain one-room red schoolhouse in Massachusetts that became famous—all because of Mary Elizabeth Sawyer . . . and her lamb.*

It was a cold day in March 1815. Nine-year-old Mary Sawyer was helping her father take care of the spring lambs. Soon she came across one that had lost its mother. It was all alone, and it looked so sweet and lost that Mary's heart went out to it at once. "Please, Papa," she begged, "may I keep this lamb and raise it as my own?" He gave her permission.

One morning a year later, Mary and her brother Nat were setting off for school. They had barely started down the path when they heard little feet scurrying behind them and a plaintive "Baaa, baaa." It was Mary's lamb, who did not want to be left behind. Mary and Nat looked at each other and said at once, "Let's take it with us."

Nat lifted the lamb up over the fence and they were on their way.

They soon reached the one-room red schoolhouse. Luckily they were the first to arrive, so no one saw them smuggle the lamb in, hide it beneath Mary's wooden desk, and cover it with a shawl. "You must be very quiet and good," whispered Mary to her lamb.

Miss Kimball, their teacher, arrived and started a fire in the fireplace. Her guest, Mr. John Roulstone, helped, noticing how the children's ink bottles were kept in a special niche by the fireplace to keep them from freezing. The rest of the children came in and took their seats. They pulled out their slates and copybooks and started their daily lessons.

In those days the entire school met in one classroom. The teacher was responsible for teaching everyone—no matter how old or young. Students would sit quietly at their desks, memorizing from the few books available, doing sums on their slates, or practicing penmanship in their copybooks. Then they would each be called on to present their work to the teacher.

Miss Kimball began to call on the children to recite what they had memorized. Soon it was Mary's turn. But as she made her way down the narrow aisle to the front of the class, the children started giggling and pointing at her. Even Miss Kimball and Mr. Roulstone couldn't keep a straight face for long. Mary's lamb had come out from under the desk and was following its beloved Mary down the aisle!

Miss Kimball did ask Mary to put the lamb out in the shed for the day. And Mr. Roulstone, to make up for laughing at her, wrote Mary the poem we have all come to know and love as "Mary Had a Little Lamb."

# Revenge on the Schoolmaster

*Mark Twain, one of our greatest American authors, often wrote about experiences from his own Missouri boyhood. Here he tells about some children who get even with a teacher who punished them harshly.*

Vacation was approaching. The schoolmaster, always severe, grew more exacting than ever, for he wanted the school to make a good showing on "Examination" day. His rod and his ferrule were seldom idle now—at least among the smaller pupils. The consequence was that the smaller boys spent their days in terror and suffering and their nights in plotting revenge. At last they conspired together and hit upon a plan that promised a dazzling victory.

On Examination Evening the schoolhouse was brilliantly lighted, and adorned with wreaths and festoons of foliage. The master sat throned in his great chair upon a raised platform, with his blackboard behind him. Three rows of benches on each side and six rows in front of him were occupied by the dignitaries of the town and by the parents of the pupils. To his left were seated the scholars who were to take part in the exercises of the evening.

The exercises began. A very little boy stood up and sheepishly recited. A shamefaced little girl lisped "Mary Had a Little Lamb," etc., got her meed of applause, and sat down flushed and excited. And so forth and so on.

Now the master, mellow almost to the verge of geniality, put his chair aside, turned his back to the audience, and began to draw a map of America on the blackboard, to exercise the geography class upon. But he made a sad business of it and a smothered titter rippled over the house. He sponged out lines and remade them; but he only distorted them more than ever, and the tittering was more pronounced.

And well it might. Over his head came a cat, suspended around the haunches by a string. As she slowly descended, she curved upward and clawed at the string, and she swung downward and clawed at the intangible air. The tittering rose higher and higher—the cat was within six inches of the absorbed teacher's head—down, down, a little lower, and she grabbed his wig with her desperate claws, clung to it, and was snatched up in an instant with her trophy!

That broke up the meeting. The boys were avenged. Vacation had come.

*From* The Adventures of Tom Sawyer *by Mark Twain*

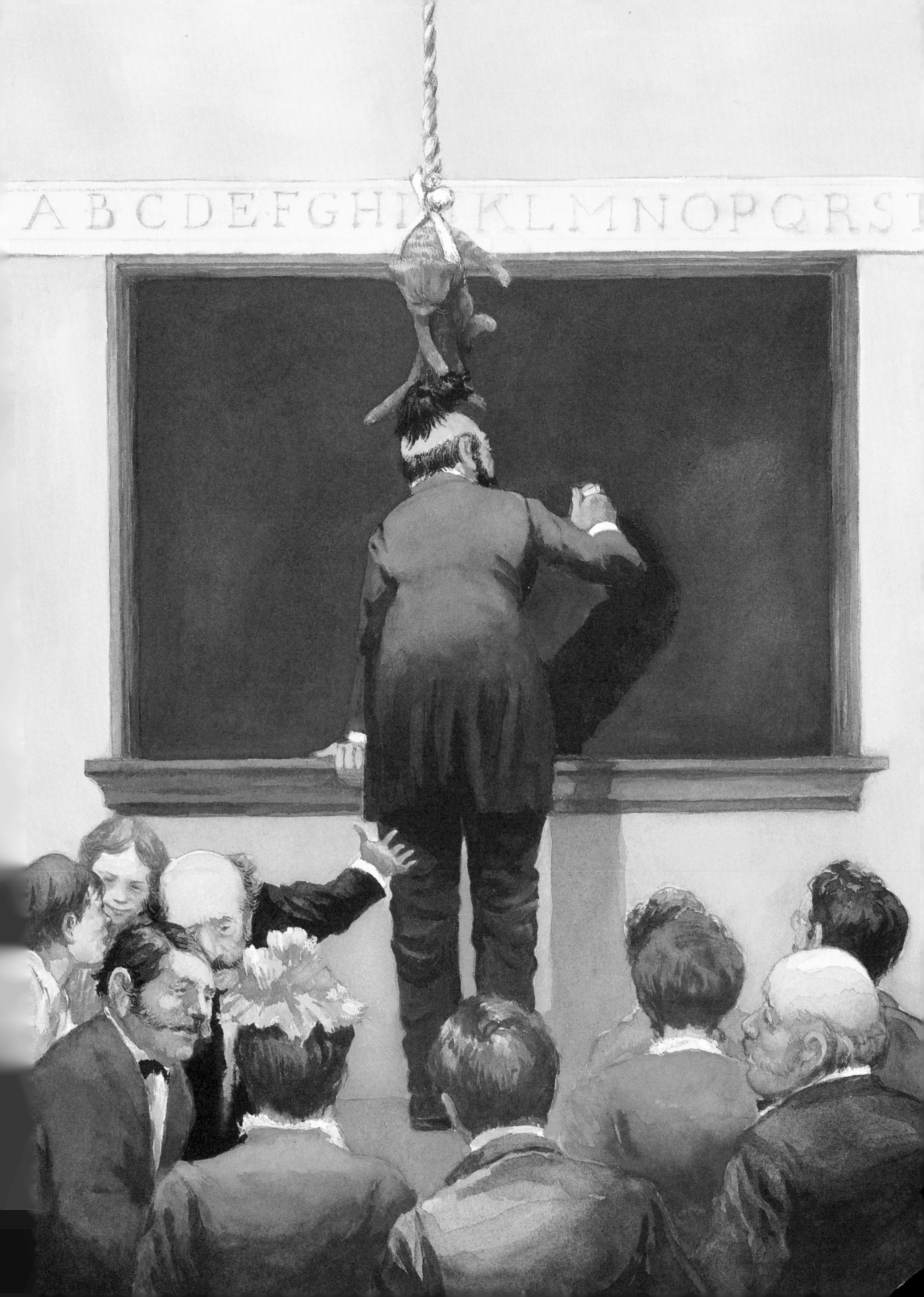
ABCDEFGHI KLMNOPQRST

# How I Learned to Read and Write

*Frederick Douglass, an abolitionist and former slave, knew that education was a step toward freedom. Even though slave children were forbidden to learn to read and write, young Frederick was clever enough to find a way to educate himself.*

I lived in Master Hugh's family about seven years. During this time, I learned to read and write. I had no regular teacher. The plan which I used was to make friends of all the little white boys whom I met in the street. As many of these as I could I converted into teachers. With their kindly aid, at different times and in different places, I finally succeeded in learning to read.

When I was sent on errands, I always took my book with me. By doing one part of my errand quickly, I found time to get a lesson before my return. I also used to carry bread with me. Plenty of bread was always in the house, and I was always welcome to it. I was much better off in this way than many of the poor white children in our neighborhood. I used to give this bread to the hungry little children I met, who, in return, would give me that more valuable bread of knowledge. I would like to give the names of two or three of those little boys, because of the gratitude and affection I have for them. But I will not name them here. For it is a serious offense to teach slaves to read in this Christian country.

I was now about twelve years old, and the thought of being a slave for life began to weigh heavily upon my heart. I looked forward to a time when it would be safe for me to escape. I comforted myself with the hope that I should one day find a good chance. Meanwhile, I would learn to write.

The idea about how I might learn to write came to me in Durgin and Bailey's shipyard. I often watched the ship carpenters there get a piece of timber ready for use. When a piece of timber was made for the larboard side of the ship, it would be marked "L." A piece for the starboard side would be marked "S." A piece for the larboard side forward would be marked "L.F." For starboard side forward, it would be marked "S.F." For larboard aft, it would be marked "L.A." and for starboard aft, it would be marked "S.A."

I soon learned the names of these letters, and what they meant when they were written on a piece of timber in the shipyard. I began to copy them, and in a short time I was able to make the four letters L, S, F, and A.

After that, when I met with any boy who I knew could write, I would tell him I could write as well as he. The next words would be "I don't believe you. Let me see you try it." I would then make the letters I had learned, and ask him to beat that. I had many lessons in writing this way which I might have never gotten otherwise. During this time, my copybook was the board fence, brick wall, and pavement; my pen and ink was a lump of chalk. With these, I learned mainly how to write.

*Adapted from* Narrative of the Life of Frederick Douglass

# HARRIET TUBMAN

*Born a slave, Harriet Tubman escaped
to freedom in her twenties. Later, she
risked her life to free hundreds of slaves
on the Underground Railroad, and so
was called the "Moses of Her People."*

She was a black American
Born a slave
She was frightened sometimes
But brave
And determined
She sang songs a lot
She was aggressive
Was angry
Was a genius
And she was kind
She was smart
Quiet
And quick
She freed about 300 slaves
And died free.

*Seth Uselman, age nine*

# A LETTER TO ABRAHAM LINCOLN

*Abraham Lincoln, our sixteenth President, is best remembered as the national leader who freed the slaves and led the North through the Civil War. But Lincoln might not have been elected President at all without the advice of a girl named Grace Bedell.*

Whenever Grace Bedell's father went to the Chautauqua County fair, he always returned with a small souvenir. One night he brought back a photograph of Abraham Lincoln. "He just might be our next President," said Grace's father.

Grace had never seen a photograph before. She studied Lincoln's picture for hours. That night, she decided to write him a letter:

*October 15, 1860*

*Dear Sir*

*I am a little girl only 11 years old, but want you should be President of the United States very much so I hope you wont think me very bold to write to such a great man as you are. I have got four brothers and part of them will vote for you any way and if you will let your whiskers grow I will try to get the rest of them to vote for you. You would look a great deal better for your face is so thin. All the ladies like whiskers and they would tease their husbands to vote for you and then you would be President.*

*Grace Bedell*

Lincoln wrote back to Grace, thanking her for the letter. But he didn't say whether or not he would follow her advice. In November 1860, he was elected President, and a few months later, he visited Westfield, New York, the town where Grace lived. People came from miles around to see him, but Lincoln was eager to meet one special person in his audience.

"Is Grace Bedell here?" he asked the crowd. She ran to him and he lifted her high, then he kissed her on both cheeks. "Look, Grace—I let my whiskers grow for you!" said the President.

# THE STORY MY GRANDMOTHER TOLD ME

*During the Civil War (1861–1865), the sadness of lives lost was felt in both the North and the South. In 1864, the North sent General William T. Sherman on a march of destruction through the state of Georgia. Here is the true story of a family who survived a visit from Sherman's army.*

"Well, Laura Anne, I was just a little girl, but old enough to know that something terrible was happening. Mother and Dad lived out from Savannah on a large farm. Dad grew everything we needed as well as cotton and tobacco. We had cows, horses, pigs, chickens—I guess about everything one could have living in the country.

"I shall always remember a particular day in 1864. One of our neighbors came riding up to the house digging the spurs in the horse's sides. My father was not home at the time but my mother came running out. The boy was waving his arms and yelling at the top of his voice, 'The Yankees are coming! General Sherman has burned up Atlanta and is on his way to Savannah. He is destroying everything in his path. Save what you can! He'll be here soon. I've got to warn the others.'

"My sister Idel had a high fever and was upstairs in her bed. Mother told everyone to take the silver and hide it under Idel's bed. She told our Mammy to sit on a sack of potatoes and spread her wide apron over it. She told Mammy's little boy to take a cow and run across the creek to a spot where he would be completely hidden.

"Mother had only a short time to make those decisions because soon there was a loud commotion as horses and soldiers filled up the yard. I was frightened and hid behind Mother's skirt.

"There was an exchange of words between the soldier in command and Mother. She told him she had a daughter quite ill upstairs who should not be disturbed, and so a soldier was placed in front of her door to keep the others from entering her room. But everything of any value was taken from the rest of the house. Some of the soldiers set fire to the grain fields while others killed the hogs and chickens.

"After the soldiers finally left, the heads of the hogs were gathered and the meat was scraped off and cooked. We ate a lot of burnt corn. I guess we were fortunate that our house wasn't burned to the ground. Many were.

"Now, Laura Anne, you won't find that story in your history books but I am sure you have read often about General Sherman's 'March to the Sea' and how he destroyed everything in his path. Well, darling, we were one of those families in his path."

*From "The Story My Grandmother Told Me"*
*by Cornelia Arvanti Erskine*

# CATTLE IN THE HAY

*The lives of pioneer children were filled with unexpected adventures. One day, when Mary and Laura Ingalls were alone on their Minnesota farm, they had to think and act quickly to save their family's winter store of hay.*

Summer was gone, winter was coming, and now it was time for Pa to make a trip to town. Here in Minnesota, town was so near that Pa would be gone only one day, and Ma was going with him.

She took Carrie, because Carrie was too little to be left far from Ma. But Mary and Laura were big girls. Mary was going on nine and Laura was going on eight, and they could stay at home and take care of everything while Pa and Ma were gone.

"Now be good girls, Laura and Mary," was the last thing Ma said. She was on the wagon seat, with Carrie beside her. Their lunch was in the wagon. Pa took up the ox goad.

"We'll be back before sundown," he promised. "Hi-oop!" he said to Pete and Bright. The big ox and the little one leaned into their yoke and the wagon started.

Slowly the wagon went away. Pa walked beside the oxen. Ma and Carrie, the wagon, and Pa all grew smaller, till they were gone into the prairie.

The prairie seemed big and empty then, but there was nothing to be afraid of. There were no wolves and no Indians. Besides, Jack stayed close to Laura. Jack was a responsible dog. He knew that he must take care of everything when Pa was away.

That morning Mary and Laura played by the creek, among the rushes. At noon they ate the corn dodgers and molasses and drank the milk that Ma had left for them. They washed their tin cups and put them away.

Then Laura wanted to play on the big rock, but Mary wanted to stay in the dugout. She said that Laura must stay there, too.

"I guess I can play where I want to!" said Laura.

Mary grabbed at her, but Laura was too quick. She darted out, and she would have run up the path, but Jack was in the way. He stood stiff, looking across the creek. Laura looked too, and she screeched, "Mary!"

The cattle were all around Pa's hay-stacks. They were eating the hay. They were tearing into the stacks with their horns, gouging out hay, eating it and trampling over it.

There would be nothing left to feed Pete and Bright and Spot in the winter-time.

Jack knew what to do. He ran growling down the steps to the foot-bridge. Pa was not there to save the hay-stacks; they must drive those cattle away.

"Oh, we can't! We can't!" Mary said, scared. But Laura ran behind Jack and Mary came after her. They went over the creek and past the spring. They came up on the prairie and now they saw the fierce, big cattle quite near. The long horns were gouging, the thick legs trampling and jostling, the wide mouths bawling.

Mary was too scared to move. Laura was too scared to stand still. She jerked Mary along. She saw a stick, and grabbed it up and ran yelling at the cattle. Jack ran at them, growling.

But they could not chase those cattle away from the hay-stacks. The cattle

ran around and around and in between the stacks, jostling and bawling, tearing off hay and trampling it. More and more hay slid off the stacks. Laura ran panting and yelling, waving her stick. The faster she ran, the faster the cattle went, black and brown and red, brindle and spotted cattle, big and with awful horns, and they would not stop wasting the hay.

Laura was hot and dizzy. Her hair unbraided and blew in her eyes. Her throat was rough from yelling, but she kept on yelling, running, and waving her stick. She was too scared to hit one of those big, horned cows. More and more hay kept coming down and faster and faster they trampled over it.

Suddenly Laura turned around and ran the other way. She faced the big red cow coming around a hay-stack.

The huge legs and shoulders and terrible horns were coming fast. Laura could not scream now. But she jumped at that cow and waved her stick. The cow tried to stop, but all the other cattle were coming behind her and she couldn't. She swerved and ran away across the ploughed ground, all the others galloping after her.

Jack and Laura and Mary chased them, farther and farther from the hay. Far into the high prairie grasses they chased those cattle.

They went back through the high grass that dragged at their trembling legs. They were glad to drink at the spring. They were glad to be in the quiet dugout and sit down to rest.

*From* On the Banks of Plum Creek *by Laura Ingalls Wilder*

# CHANO'S FIRST BUFFALO HUNT

*Chano, the son of a Lakota Sioux chieftain, grew up on the Great Plains in the late 1800s. He became a true Indian brave on his first buffalo hunt.*

Chano felt excited and strong as he rode with the men. Two or three miles from camp they saw hundreds of animals. To Chano it looked like a huge herd.

The hunters circled the herd until they were downwind from them, and keeping behind high ground, managed to get within a few hundred feet before they were discovered. The whole herd wheeled and stampeded away from the hunters.

For a moment Chano was stunned by the thunderous roar made by the hundreds of pounding hooves and the big cloud of dust that was raised. Before Chano realized it, his pony had worked himself right into the herd. Buffalo rubbed against his legs on each side. Their great bodies pressed around him and he could feel their heat.

Chano was a little frightened at first. He knew if his pony tripped or if he should fall off his back, he would be trampled to death.

He took heart as he noticed his pony was enjoying the hunt. The

pony flattened down his ears and with a snort of delight raced along with the herd.

Chano, riding skillfully, waited until he came abreast of a fine yearling cow. Fitting an arrow to his bow he took careful aim and let it go. It struck her right behind the shoulder. He shot a second arrow and this time she dropped. He looked down at her, his first buffalo, killed with the bow and arrow he had made with his own hands. His heart sang. He raised his hands to the sky and gave thanks to Wakan-tanka.

When he dismounted, he took his hunting knife and began to skin the buffalo. He cut the choicest portions of the meat and tied it up in a piece of the fresh skin. The heart, liver, and kidneys he wrapped separately. They were a special present for his aunt and uncle.

On his ride back to camp Chano sang his first brave song. He was happy that he had not been afraid, that he had killed his first buffalo, that he too could join with the other men of the tribe in hunting.

Chano reached camp long after the others had returned. He washed himself and then entered the tipi. He sat down and looked at the evening meal, roast buffalo ribs. He ate heartily.

After they had all eaten, Chano's uncle asked about the hunt. Chano replied that everyone got at least one buffalo and some two or three.

"Did you get one?" asked his uncle with a smile.

For an answer Chano went outside and dragged in the big bundles of meat. His aunt and uncle were pleased with his modesty and even more pleased with the delicacies he had brought back for them.

Iron Plume immediately sent a crier through the camp to tell everyone of Chano's success on his first buffalo hunt. He also invited them to a feast in Chano's honor the next day.

It is an old custom to give a feast in honor of a great deed done by a loved one. It was a fine feast. Everyone ate, sang, and danced. Many said how brave it was for such a young boy to bring down a buffalo all by himself. In his heart Chano sang his brave song again.

When the feast was over and they were alone again, Iron Plume called Chano to him and told him that his father would be coming to take him home sometime during the next few days.

Iron Plume said, "And I cannot return to him what he brought me."

"Why?" said Chano. "I'm here just the same."

"No, my son," replied Iron Plume, "Tasinagi brought me a boy and I return to him a mighty hunter." Then he smiled at Chano.

This time Chano sang his brave song not only in his heart but aloud so that his aunt and uncle could hear him. He was a man—no longer a boy.

*From* Tonweya and the Eagles
*by Rosebud Yellow Robe*

# WE CHASED
# BUTTERFLIES

*There were many lessons that a Crow Indian
boy needed to learn before he became a man.
This poem describes the very first lesson.*

We chased butterflies to give us endurance
in running. After we caught one, we rubbed our hearts
with its wings, saying,
"Oh, Butterfly, lend me your grace and swiftness!"
That was a boy's first lesson.

*Plenty-Coups, Chief of the Crows*

# IS THERE A SANTA CLAUS?

*Virginia O'Hanlon wanted to know whether or not to believe in Santa Claus, so she wrote to the "Question and Answer" column of* The New York Sun. *The answer that appeared in the newspaper settled the question for all time.*

*Dear Editor:*
*I am 8 years old. Some of my little friends say there is no Santa Claus. Papa says "If you see it in the* Sun *it's so."*
*Please tell me the truth; is there a Santa Claus?*

*Virginia O'Hanlon*

Virginia, your little friends are wrong. They have been affected by the skepticism of a skeptical age. They do not believe except they see. They think that nothing can be which is not comprehensible by their little minds. All minds, Virginia, whether they be men's or children's, are little. In this great universe of ours man is a mere insect, an ant, in his intellect, as compared with the boundless world about him, as measured by the intelligence capable of grasping the whole of truth and knowledge.

Yes, Virginia, there is a Santa Claus. He exists as certainly as love and generosity and devotion exist, and you know that they abound and give to your life its highest beauty and joy. Alas! how dreary would be the world if there were no Santa Claus! It would be as dreary as if there were no Virginias. There would be no childlike faith then, no poetry, no romance to make tolerable this existence. We should have no enjoyment, except in sense and sight. The eternal light with which childhood fills the world would be extinguished.

Not believe in Santa Claus! You might as well not believe in fairies! You might get your papa to hire men to watch in all the chimneys on Christmas Eve to catch Santa Claus, but even if they did not see Santa Claus coming down, what would that prove? Nobody sees Santa Claus, but that is no sign that there is no Santa Claus. The most real things in the world are those that neither children nor men can see.

No Santa Claus! Thank God, he lives, and he lives forever. A thousand years from now, Virginia, nay, ten times ten thousand years from now, he will continue to make glad the heart of childhood.

*From* The New York Sun, *September 21, 1897*

# In 1900 to 1929 . . .

Buffalo Bill's Wild West Show toured the world.

Favorite toys and games included Crayola crayons, the Teddy Bear, Raggedy Ann, Kewpie dolls, and crossword puzzles.

Favorite treats were animal crackers, hot dogs, Popsicles, and potato chips.

At home, children were entertained by radios, phonographs, and player pianos.

The Boy Scouts, Girl Scouts, and Camp Fire Girls were founded.

In 1927, Babe Ruth hit 60 home runs, a record unbroken for thirty-four years. Baseball cards were collected and traded.

Football became a popular sport.

Favorite children's books included *The Wonderful Wizard of Oz, The Tale of Peter Rabbit, Winnie-the-Pooh,* and *The Little Engine That Could.*

Charlie Chaplin and Tom Mix were popular stars of silent movies.

The Wright brothers launched the first airplane at Kitty Hawk, North Carolina.

# "LOOK, AMERICA!":
## Oral Histories From Ellis Island

*Ellis Island in New York Harbor was the first stop for 16 million immigrants who came from Europe from 1892 to 1954. Immigration officials checked passports and gave medical exams to would-be citizens before they were given permission to stay in the United States. Ellis Island is now a museum dedicated to the many stories of coming to America.*

That was the first time I saw the Statue of Liberty, when I was standing on deck. And I had a hat on and the wind came along and took my hat off and I said to my mother in Italian, "Mama, there goes my hat!" And I said to her, "Look at the lady, the lady over there!"

*Joseph Allatin emigrated from Italy in 1894 at the age of six.*

They said the streets were paved with gold and all you had to do is wish for candy and open your mouth and it would drop right in. And that there were Indians here and they would cut off your hair and make wigs out of it, and all kinds of things like that.

*Margot Starck emigrated from Germany in 1920 at the age of eleven.*

First of all, you got off the boat, you went onto this gangplank that went into the building, and you walked into narrow little trails where there were iron gates in front of you. So they opened up and let so many people through, and then they clanged shut. And when you looked and you saw all of these gates, you really thought, "Boy, we're in a prison."

*Charlotte Youngs emigrated from Germany in 1925 at the age of eleven.*

They knew that children had to be occupied, and there was a place where we went to play. And I remember we each got a toy, and I got my one and only doll that I ever owned, and it was made of a linoleum material. It wasn't even a doll that did anything, but I was so thrilled to have it. That was an exciting thing to have, your own doll.

*Mary Nerstad emigrated from the Ukraine in 1926 at the age of eight.*

I turned seven after we got here and they put me in the first grade. I didn't know the language and every time the teacher even looked at me I would start to cry, because I was afraid and I didn't know what she was saying. But there was one little girl that I'll never forget. When it was recess time, this one girl came and put her arm around my shoulder. She didn't say anything, she just took me outside, stayed with me during recess, and when recess was over she brought me back to my seat in school. That girl, I'll never forget her.

*Birgitta Fichter emigrated from Sweden in 1924 at the age of six.*

I remember the first night we went to Times Square and my father took us to a cafeteria and I'd never seen so much food. The trays were just not big enough to hold everything. We had a marvelous dinner and after dinner we went to the Astor Theater and saw *The Great Dictator* with Charlie Chaplin. That was a marvelous introduction really because a film like that would not have been seen in Europe, especially at that time. And seeing the spoof on Hitler made us aware that finally we were in the land of freedom.

*Paul H. Laric emigrated from Yugoslavia in 1940 at the age of fourteen.*

# THE STREET

*For a city child growing up at the turn of the century, everything that was exciting and fun was happening outside—in the street.*

Children owned the streets in a way unthinkable to city children of today. There were a few parks, but too distant to be of any use, and so the street was the common playground.

The separation of boys and girls so rigidly carried out in the public school also held on the street; boys played with boys, girls with girls.

Except on rare occasions, we girls played only girls' games. Tagging after us sometimes were our little brothers and sisters whom we were supposed to mind, but that was no great hardship or hindrance. We would toss them our beanbags, little cloth containers filled with cherry pits.

"Now see that you play here on the stoop or you won't get any ice cream when the hoky-poky man comes along." The hope of getting that penny's worth of ice cream dished out on a bit of brown paper was sufficient to quell any revolt on the part of our little charges.

Mama didn't like me to play potsy. She thought it "disgraceful" to mark up our sidewalk with chalk for our lines and boxes; besides, hopping on one foot and pushing the thick piece of tin, I managed to wear out a pair of shoes in a few weeks!

I obeyed her wishes in my own way, by playing farther down the street and marking up someone else's sidewalk.

Neither my friends nor I played much with dolls. Most families had at least one baby on hand; we girls had plenty of opportunity to shower upon the baby brothers or sisters the tenderness and love that would otherwise have been given to dolls.

Besides, dolls were expensive. We often stopped to look at the shop windows on Grand Street. The dolls were gorgeous: blue-eyed bits of perfection dressed in unimaginable splendor. Next to them were miniature trunks filled with clothes, from tiny white leather shoes to poke bonnets.

Regardless of season, the favorite game of both boys and girls was "prisoner's base." We lined up on opposite sides of the curb, our numbers evenly divided, representing two enemy camps.

One side turned its back to invite a surprise attack. Stealthily a contestant advanced and either

safely reached the "enemy" and captured a "prisoner," or, if caught, became a "prisoner." Shouts of defiance could be heard a block off when someone was captured. When a sufficient number of prisoners had been taken, a tug of war followed to rescue them.

Trucks and brewery wagons lumbered by. We looked upon them merely as an unnecessary interference with the progress of our game. Sometimes, to be sure, accidents occurred, but they were rare; either we were very fleet of foot or the drivers obligingly slowed their horses.

*From* Horsecars and Cobblestones
*by Sophie Ruskay*

# TORCHLIGHT PARADE

*Today, television brings us up-to-the-minute news. But back in the 1920s, Dorothy Ann McVay was thrilled to be at the center of an exciting news event when a hometown hero named Warren G. Harding was elected President of the United States.*

Marion, Ohio—1920

I live in President Harding's town. During the campaign there was no little excitement, and on election night there was a big celebration. There were over twelve thousand people in the streets, and also many delegations from all over Ohio and neighboring States. They had a torchlight parade, and many thousand people took part. Later that evening we all went out to the Harding home. The President-elect made a short speech.

They have changed the name of our high school from Marion High School to Harding High School.

Now that the campaign is over I suppose most of the excitement is over too, but I think Marion will be, from now on, far more important than it ever was before.

*From a letter to* St. Nicholas *magazine from Dorothy Ann McVay*

47

# WHERE EVERYTHING IS FREE

*Leaving their homeland was hard for some immigrant children. But the Russian children in this story, who arrived in New York City at the turn of the century, soon saw how good their life in a new country would be.*

At our first meal my father gave us several kinds of food, ready to eat, without any cooking, from little tin cans that had printing all over them. He also attempted to introduce us to a queer, slippery kind of fruit, which he called "banana" but had to give it up for the time being.

After the meal, he had better luck with an odd piece of furniture on runners, which he called "rocking chair." There were five of us newcomers, and we found five different ways of getting into the American perpetual motion machine, and as many ways of getting out of it.

In our flat there was no bathtub. So in the evening of the first day my father led us to the public baths. As we moved along in a little parade, I was delighted with the brightly lit streets. So many lamps, and they burned until morning, my father said, and so people did not need to carry lanterns.

In America, then, everything was free, as we had heard in Russia. Light was free; the streets were as bright as a synagogue on a holy day. Music was free; for we had been serenaded, to our delight, by a brass band of many pieces, in the square at Union Place.

Education was free. My father had often written to us about his chief hope for us children, the core of American opportunity, the treasure that no thief could touch, not even misfortune or poverty. It was the one thing that he was able to promise us when he sent for us; surer, safer than bread or shelter.

On our second day I was thrilled to learn what this freedom of education meant. A little girl from across the alley came and offered to take us to school. My father was out, but we five children had learned a few words of English by this time. We knew the word *school.* We understood.

This child, who had never seen us till yesterday, and who was not much better dressed than we, was able to offer us the freedom of the schools! The doors stood open for every one of us. The smallest child could show us the way.

*Adapted from* The Promised Land
*by Mary Antin*

# THE COAL PICKERS

*The rights of American children were not always protected by the government. Until the child labor laws of 1924 and 1938, boys and girls as young as nine worked long hours for pennies a day at hard, dangerous jobs in mines, mills, and factories. They didn't go to school and had little time to play.*

In a little room in this big, black shed—a room not twenty feet square—forty boys are picking their lives away. The floor of the room is an inclined plane, and a stream of coal pours constantly in. They work here, in this little black hole, all day and every day, trying to keep cool in summer, trying to keep warm in winter, picking away among the black coals, bending over till their little spines are curved, never saying a word all the livelong day.

These little fellows go to work in this cold dreary room at seven o'clock in the morning and work till it is too dark to see any longer.

For this they get one dollar to three dollars a week. Not three boys in this roomful could read or write. Shut in from everything that is pleasant, with no chance to learn, with no knowledge of what is going on about them, with nothing to do but work, grinding their little lives away in this dusty room, they are no more than the wire screens that separate the great lumps of coal from the small. They had no games; when their day's work is done they are too tired for that. They know nothing but the difference between slate and coal.

*From* The Labor Standard, *1877*

50

# THE GOLF LINKS

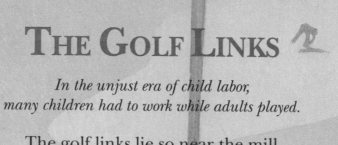

*In the unjust era of child labor,*
*many children had to work while adults played.*

The golf links lie so near the mill
That almost every day
The laboring children can look out
And see the men at play.

*Sarah N. Cleghorn*

# THE WAR ENDED ON LIBERTY STREET

*The day World War I ended, November 11, 1918, was an important day in American history. Hildegarde Dolson made her own history that day by becoming the first news*girl.

"Come on, kid," the red-haired boy told me. He and four other boys escorted me through the alley to Liberty Street. By that time the entire block was jammed with shouting, happy people, but the boys formed a sort of flying wedge, to get me across the street and over in front of the Exchange Bank. "This is where you stand and sell," my red-haired patron said. "It's the best place in town." Another of my new friends said proudly, "I'll betcha she's the first girl that ever sold papers."

"Don't forget to yell," the red-haired boy told me. "Just holler 'Armistice—read all about the Armistice.'" After all the boys had

gone, I stood in a flushed, dreamy fever of excitement, watching the people. There were church bells ringing and factory whistles tooting continuously. The town band marched up the street and stopped almost beside me, to play "Hail, Hail, the Gang's All Here." Any cars that could get through the crowds of people in the street were proceeding slowly, with bleating horns to add to the din. I remember gaping at a man sitting out on the front radiator of one of these moving automobiles shouting, "We licked the Fritzies."

A group of high-school students formed a snake dance and weaved down the street, yelling. Somewhere behind me, firecrackers were going off. My head was light and floating with the excitement and noise. I watched grownups hugging each other on the sidewalk, but the thing that impressed me most was to see them running around outdoors on a cold day without their hats or coats.

Everybody must have felt that a little girl selling papers was one of the gay, crazy things that could be expected to happen on Armistice Day.

There must have been another wonderful, dizzying hour while I stood there in front of the bank, handing out papers and collecting more money than I had ever seen in my life. Several of the newsboys brought me more *Herald*s, and I paid them nonchalantly from the money stuffing my pockets.

It must have been almost five o'clock when I saw my father coming up Liberty Street, through the thinning crowd. "Father," I called. "Look, Father, I'm selling papers."

I have never seen my father so completely dumbfounded. As I hauled out handfuls of money to show him, he kept shaking his head in a dazed sort of way. "You said I could," I reminded him. "You said I could the day the war ended."

When he'd recovered his wind, my father said, "Well, we'd better go home now."

In the excitement of my homecoming, nobody had the heart to scold me, and Bobby [my brother] was even allowed to eat gumdrops before dinner.

*From* We Shook the Family Tree
*by Hildegarde Dolson*

53

# SPECS TOPORCER

*It seems as if baseball has always been America's favorite pastime! For this young boy, baseball was the best part of being an American. His love of the game, his talent, and his persistence led Specs Toporcer from the streets of New York to the Big Leagues!*

To begin at the beginning, I was born in New York City in 1899. We lived on 77th Street between 1st and 2nd Avenues, above the shop where Dad made shoes and boots.

When I was ten years old I started making frequent afternoon excursions up to the Polo Grounds, at 157th Street and 8th Avenue, to see the Giants play. This meant a five-mile walk each way from our home on 77th Street. It wasn't so bad. Only took me an hour and a half each way. Dad was able to give me a weekly allowance of only one cent—yes, one cent—so I didn't have enough money for street cars or subways, and of course I couldn't pay my way into the ball park either.

Fortunately, I was able to see my heroes from a perch on Coogan's Bluff, a hill situated behind the home-plate area of the grandstand. An open space below the roof of the stadium made it possible for me, and for others crowded together on the rocky hill, to peek at part of what was happening on the field.

When I was 13 years old, I got a job posting scores in an old-fashioned corner saloon. The scores would come in on a Western Union ticker tape, and I'd proudly write them on a large blackboard in the back room of the saloon. Games started at four o'clock in the afternoon in those days, so even when school was in session it was easy for me to get there on time.

During the regular season, the ticker tape provided only the inning-by-inning scores and the pitchers and catchers. At World Series time, though, a complete play-by-play came over the ticker, and instead of just writing the scores on the blackboard, the management had me stand on a platform and read the tape in a loud voice. This was 1912, remember, the Giants versus the Red Sox, and the saloon was jammed to overflowing with hundreds inside and out eagerly following each game's progress.

Unfortunately, that was the year Fred Snodgrass, one of my favorites, dropped a fly ball in the tenth inning of the last game, after which the Red Sox scored two unearned runs to come from behind and win the Series. I broke down and found it almost impossible to announce the tragic events to the hushed crowd. After it was all over, I sat on the platform silently reading and re-reading the doleful news on the tape, as though repeated reading would erase the awful words.

When I was in the seventh grade, our history teacher decided to organize a school baseball team. I was overjoyed and eagerly showed up for tryouts—only to be turned down because I was too frail and wore eyeglasses. In those days, nobody played ball with eyeglasses on.

I was heartbroken at being rejected, but I persisted in following the school team around from game to game anyway. One day I got a lucky break: only eight of our players showed up for a game and I was the only rooter from our school who was on hand to cheer the team on. So our history teacher-manager put me in center field, probably because it was the least desirable position.

As things turned out, though, I had no accidents, was lucky enough to make a sparkling one-handed catch, and also contributed two hits. From then on, I was a regular!

*From* The Glory of Their Times
*by Lawrence S. Ritter*

# In 1930 to 1949 . . .

Favorite talking movies were *The Wizard of Oz; Frankenstein; Tarzan, the Ape Man;* Marx Brothers movies; Shirley Temple movies; and Walt Disney movies, such as *Snow White and the Seven Dwarfs, Bambi,* and *Dumbo.*

Favorite radio shows were "Little Orphan Annie," "The Lone Ranger," "The Shadow," and "Fibber McGee and Molly."

Favorite toys included Dy-dee dolls (a diapered baby doll), jacks, jump rope, and marbles.

Comic book heroes included Buck Rogers, Dick Tracy, Popeye, Batman, and Superman.

Mickey Mouse won America's heart in 1935 when he appeared in his first color cartoon, *The Band Concert.*

Favorite treats were Twinkies, chocolate bars, peanut butter, corn chips, ice-cream sodas, and charlotte russe.

America entered World War II in 1941.

Favorite children's books were *National Velvet, Little House in the Big Woods, The Story of Babar, Mary Poppins,* and *And to Think I Saw It on Mulberry Street.*

# PLAYHOUSE MEMORIES

*In difficult times, a favorite toy or game is especially precious to a child. This little girl's playhouse helped make growing up in the Depression a bit easier.*

After we lost our home during the Depression, we moved around a lot, sharecropping from one farm to another. I know this must have been hectic for our precious mama. She'd have to pack up our meager belongings, which Daddy always moved in a two-horse or mule wagon. But to us children it was great fun. Especially exciting for me was the pleasure of finding a new location for my most beloved playhouse.

The spot had to be in just the right location. I preferred that this place be rather close to our home, if possible, in a shaded area by the edge of the woods. I'd sweep the ground perfectly clean, putting planks all around for the borders of my playhouse. Then I'd put more planks across molasses buckets for my tables, using buckets for my chairs also. I'd use pine straw for my bed, and green leaves pinned together with broom straw for my "just playing" clothes.

*From* Growing Up in the Depression
*by Estelle Barlow*

# SHIRLEY TEMPLE: *Child Star*

*Born in 1928, Shirley Temple was a world-famous movie star by the time she was six years old. As an adult, she was again world-famous as a representative to the United Nations and as a United States ambassador. Here she talks about her everyday life as a young film star.*

On the days when I am making a picture, I get up very early in the morning. The night before, Mother brushes my hair and curls it over her fingers and fastens it with bobby pins. Then in the morning she just has to brush it out.

Then we eat breakfast and hurry off to the studio.

Mother tells me the story of the picture we are making, before I play in any scenes. They give her a big book at the studio. It is called "the script."

She tells me the story and what I have to do. Then she reads my part to me and I learn the words. Mother reads the speeches of the other players, and tells me which is my "cue." That means, when I have to say my part.

I learn all my speeches before the picture is begun.

At the studio, I get dressed for the part, and then we "rehearse." Then the director says, "Everybody quiet. We'll take it now." Then we take it. I like that. I always remember my

58

speeches, especially the long ones. They are easier than the little short ones.

At the studio, they have fixed a little bungalow just for Mother and me. It is a real little house, with flowers growing around it. And there is a bird house in front.

There is a little kitchen, where Mother cooks my lunch, and there is a bedroom, where I have my nap. One room is a schoolroom, with a desk and blackboard and maps and everything. I have lessons every day. I know my numbers and can write my name and I am learning to read in a pretty primer.

I love my little house and I'd like to stay there all the time, all night even. But if Mother and I stayed there, we'd invite Daddy and the boys to come to see us.

The boys are my two brothers, George and Jack. Jack is in college. George is fourteen years old and he says he would like to play in pictures. But I don't think he would like it, unless he could be a cowboy.

Of course I have fun at home, too. I love to play with dolls. The doll I like best is named Dorothy. But the thing I want most is a dog! I want a Scottie. They are so cute looking up at you and listening to everything you say. Oh, I do want one!

*From* Child Life *magazine, 1935*

# MY TRIP TO THE WORLD'S FAIR, 1939

*Millions flocked to the 1939 World's Fair in New York City to see wonders of the future, such as television and products made of plastic. Anna Litowinska was one visitor who would never forget her day at the fair.*

We took the Hudson Tubes to New York. Then we got on the subway. I wore my new spring coat. I held on to Papa's hand as tight as I could. I didn't want to get lost.

I was excited and scared. The Fair was bigger than I ever expected. I was afraid Papa wouldn't remember the way back because the Fair was so big. It went on and on. The Trylon and Perisphere stood up high. They were so enormous. One was like a ball and the other was like a skinny pyramid.

People were everywhere. Food was almost everywhere. Papa went to the Polish pavilion and ate Polish food. The pavilion was open like a merry-go-round. A man gave me a Heinz pickle pin. It is green and one inch long.

We brought our lunch. Mama had made ham sandwiches for us to eat. She had to stay home with the baby. It was nice being with Papa. He bought us ice cream.

I liked walking around. There was so much to see. I saw a robot at the G.E. World of Tomorrow pavilion. We rode on the little railroad. I liked it a lot. Papa took a picture of me in front of the Ukrainian pavilion. There were pavilions from all the different countries.

I went to the telephone exhibit too. I also saw some strange objects like a box with moving pictures. Papa said that we were seeing things of the future.

On the way home it was hard to talk. My mind was so full. I wished I could live the day all over again. There are lots of countries in the world. I hope some day to visit one of them.

"Papa," I said, "do you think I could save up and go to the Ukraine?"

He smiled. "It's possible." Papa had been born there.

Papa knew the way home. He didn't forget. Why did I think he might?

I wish there was a World's Fair every year.

*By Anna Litowinska, age eleven*

# THE LITTLE ORPHAN ANNIE SECRET DECODER PIN

*In the 1930s and 1940s, before the Age of Television, children listened to radio programs featuring popular characters of the day, like the Shadow and the Lone Ranger. The young radio audience used their imaginations to join in the adventures of these fearless heroes.*

Every day when I was a kid I'd drop anything I was doing, no matter what it was, and tear like a blue streak through the alleys, over fences, under porches, through secret short-cuts, to get home not a second too late for the magic time. My breath rattling in wheezy gasps, sweating profusely from my long cross-country run, I'd sit glassy-eyed and expectant before our Crosley Notre Dame Cathedral model radio.

I was never disappointed. At exactly five-fifteen, just as dusk was gathering, the magic notes of an unforgettable theme song came rasping out of our Crosley:

> *"Who's that little chatterbox . . . ?*
> *The one with curly golden locks . . .*
> *Who do I see . . . ?*
> *It's Little Orphan Annie."*

Ah, they don't write tunes like that any more. There was one particularly brilliant line that dealt with Sandy, Little Orphan Annie's Airedale sidekick. Who could forget it?

> *"'Arf' goes Sandy."*

I think it was Sandy more than anyone else that drew me to the "Little Orphan Annie" radio program. Dogs in our neighborhood never went "Arf."

Little Orphan Annie lived in this great place called Tompkins Corners. There were people called Joe Corntassle and Uncle Andy. They were always chasing jewel thieves or pirates, neither of which we had in Indiana.

Immediately after the nightly adventure on would come a guy named Pierre André, the *definitive* radio announcer.

"FELLAS AND GALS. GET SET FOR A MEETING OF THE LITTLE ORPHAN ANNIE SECRET CIRCLE!"

His voice boomed out of the Crosley like some monster, maniacal pipe organ played by the Devil himself.

"OKAY, KIDS. TIME TO GET OUT YOUR SECRET DECODER PIN. TIME FOR ANOTHER

SECRET MESSAGE DIRECT FROM LITTLE ORPHAN ANNIE TO MEMBERS OF THE LITTLE ORPHAN ANNIE SECRET CIRCLE."

I got no pin. A member of an Out Group at the age of seven. And the worst kind of an Out Group. I am living in a non-Ovaltine-drinking neighborhood.

"ALL RIGHT. SET YOUR PINS TO B-7. SEVEN . . . TWENTY-TWO . . . NINETEEN . . . EIGHT . . . **FORTY-NINE** . . . SIX . . . THIRTEEN . . . **THREE**! . . . TWENTY-TWO . . . ONE. OKAY, FELLAS AND GALS, OVER AND **OUT**."

Then—silence. The show was over and you had a feeling that out there in the darkness all over the country there were millions of kids—decoding.

*From* In God We Trust, All Others Pay Cash
*by Jean Shepherd*

# GROWING UP IN WORLD WAR II

*The battles of World War II were fought far away from America, but all Americans were affected. Even children made sacrifices and did their best to help with the war effort.*

"We interrupt this broadcast for a special bulletin: Japanese planes bombed Pearl Harbor this morning."

Where was Pearl Harbor? Would the Japanese bomb us next? I was seven years old when I heard this announcement in December 1941. This is what I remember of World War II.

Early in the war, blackouts (night air-raid drills) plunged my neighborhood into pitch-dark silence. It was scary until I realized that Japan and Germany were oceans away from Ohio.

When I was eight, the U.S. Army set up a temporary training camp in a nearby inn. We played on the camp's obstacle course, scaled its stout walls, and swung across deep ditches on ropes, enjoying the course a lot more than the trainees did.

As children, we helped in the war effort by collecting scrap metal to be recycled into ammunition. In those days, there was enough brass in thirty empty lipstick tubes to make twenty cartridges. Tin cans were another source of metal. I prepared each can for scrap drives at school by rinsing it, peeling off its label, removing both ends, sticking the ends into the cylinder, and hammering the cylinder flat.

We also bought War Stamps at school for twenty-five cents each. I pasted each stamp in an album whose cover ordered, "Save to win."

Overseas products vanished "for the duration" (of the war). At home, factories produced war goods, so cars had to last "for the duration," as did shoes. My friends and I minded the bubble gum shortage the most, and rumors of a Fleer "Dubble Bubble" shipment sent us racing to the candy store.

The government also rationed food. Each civilian, kids included, had a ration book containing stamps, or "points," as the value units were called. Canned goods, for instance, not only cost money, but also "blue points." Sugar cost lots of points. Chocolate was scarce, but every year I dreamed of a chocolate birthday cake. Every year my grandmother baked me a gingerbread.

Molasses or honey replaced sugar, but most food substitutes were not as tasty. I especially remember the butter substitute: It looked like lard. Watching Grandma mix yellow food

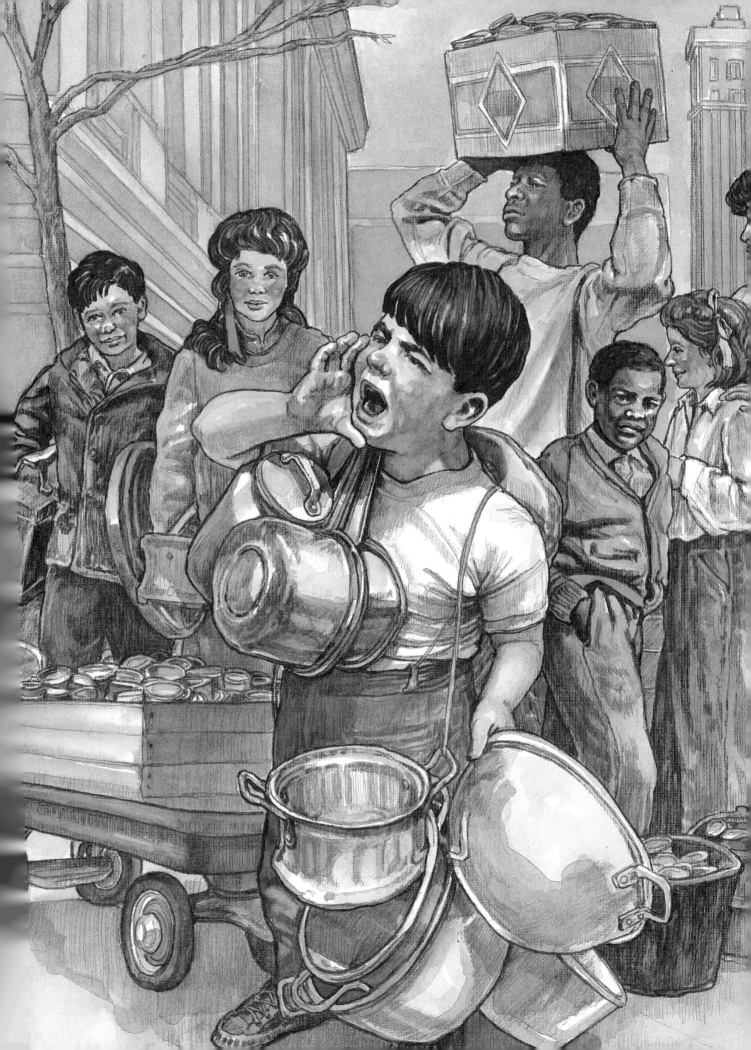

coloring into this yukky white stuff put me off margarine for years.

Saturdays we went to the movies at the Ohio Theater. Tickets cost ten cents, and popcorn was five cents a bag. Usually the Ohio ran a double feature (two movies), a cartoon, and a newsreel.

Newsreels were our version of today's television news. They showed scenes from the war, featured movie stars selling War Bonds, and introduced Rosie the Riveter, who symbolized the women who had assumed traditional male jobs "for the duration."

Comedy radio programs such as "Fibber McGee and Molly" were fun because they allowed you to create each scene in your mind. We laughed every week when Fibber McGee opened the door of his famous overstuffed closet, starting an avalanche of sounds, as basketballs, birdcages, and whatever else you could imagine bounced, tumbled, and dribbled out. I recognized radio newscasters Edward R. Murrow and H. V. Kaltenborn by voice.

One hot August day when I was ten, we were playing in the Clarks' side yard. Mrs. Clark burst onto the porch, all excited, waving her arms. "Hey, kids!" she whooped. "Paree is free! Paree is free!" With the Nazis driven out of Paris, we thought the war would be over by Christmas.

*From "Growing Up in World War II"*
*by Priscilla M. Harding*

# In the 1950s . . .

Favorite TV shows were "Howdy Doody," "Davy Crockett," "The Mickey Mouse Club," "Captain Kangaroo," "Kukla, Fran and Ollie," and "Lassie."

Popular styles were saddle shoes, flared skirts, ponytails for girls; crew cuts, blue jeans, letter sweaters for boys.

Fun fads were Hula Hoops, 3-D movies, drive-in restaurants and movie theaters, bowling, Ping-Pong.

Favorite children's books were *The Cat in the Hat*, *Charlotte's Web*, *Madeline*, *Curious George*, *Eloise*, and *Old Yeller*.

More than 1 billion comic books were sold annually. Favorite comic characters included Archie, Dennis the Menace, and Casper the Friendly Ghost.

The first major wave of UFO sightings swept the nation in 1952.

Favorite movies were Disney's *Cinderella*, *Peter Pan*, and *Lady and the Tramp*.

Disneyland opened on July 17, 1955, in Anaheim, California.

Elvis Presley was the most popular singer in America.

# OUR NEW TV SET

*The first television sets were sold in the late 1940s. By 1954, more than half of American homes had one. Today, we take television for granted. But back then, when the new TV first arrived, it was an exciting family event.*

My best friend's family had a TV set two years before us. She told me all the shows she watched and sometimes I watched with her. I was afraid we'd never get one. My father thought TV was a passing whim. He didn't believe it had staying power.

It was baseball that made my father succumb, I think. Games were now televised, he heard. Finally my father announced at dinner one night that a set was coming. My mother was thrilled. She could watch "Kraft Television Theatre."

"When?" I asked. "How soon?"

My father wasn't certain about the delivery date. But one afternoon I came home from school and in our living room stood a tall and funny-looking wooden box with a very small screen. The TV set had arrived. It was turned on and Mom and Dad were sitting up close. I pulled up a chair to join them.

"Can I watch 'Howdy Doody' when it comes on?" I asked. I knew the time already.

"Of course," they said together.

The "Howdy Doody" show became an important part of my daily routine. Only an absolute emergency, like a blizzard, or a trip to the dentist, could make me miss it. When it was "Howdy Doody" time, it was my time, too. The clown Clarabell and grumpy Mr. Bluster were so much fun to watch. I wondered if Clarabell—who only squeezed a horn to say "yes" or "no"—would ever speak. It was a live show and there was a live audience of kids called the Peanut Gallery. I always wished I could be there.

I loved "Superman," too, and never missed a show. Could Superman possibly be Clark Kent? I wondered.

We all watched the Groucho Marx quiz show, "You Bet Your Life." Groucho had that strange mustache and a long cigar. He was funny, and if the contestant said the secret word a rubber duck fell down and hit him on the head. I always waited to see that duck.

In 1955, when I was eight years old, "The Mickey Mouse Club" appeared. I sang along with the opening tune each day as the Mouseketeers marched across the screen and said their names. I wrote a long letter to my favorite Mouseketeer, Annette Funicello. She even answered me, which was pretty amazing, since she got six thousand fan letters a month.

The TV set was magical. It was amazing. All sorts of people came into our house. TV made me feel as if I was always traveling to new places and meeting new people. I couldn't get enough of it!

By the time I reached high school, my parents had put the set in the cold basement so I wouldn't watch it so much. But when the time came to watch one of my favorite shows, I loyally put on my winter coat and went downstairs. It seemed a small sacrifice to make.

*By Bebe Charles*

# CHANCLAS

*Family celebrations are happy times for young and old alike. This story tells about a special night for Esperanza Cordero, a young girl growing up in the Hispanic quarter of Chicago in the 1950s.*

It's me—Mama, Mama said. I open up and she's there with bags and big boxes, the new clothes and, yes, she's got the socks and a new slip with a little rose on it and a pink and white striped dress. What about the shoes? I forgot. Too late now. I'm tired. Whew!

Six-thirty already and my little cousin's baptism is over. All day waiting, the door locked, don't open up for nobody, and I don't till Mama gets back and buys everything except the shoes.

Now Uncle Nacho is coming in his car, and we have to hurry to get to Precious Blood Church quick because that's where the baptism party is, in the basement rented for today for dancing and tamales and everyone's kids running all over the place.

Mama dances, laughs, dances. All of a sudden, Mama is sick. I fan her hot face with a paper plate. Too many tamales, but Uncle Nacho says too many this and tilts his thumb to his lips.

Everybody laughing except me, because I'm wearing the new dress, pink and white with stripes, and new underclothes and new socks and the old saddle shoes I wear to school, brown and white, the kind I get every September because they last long and they do. My feet scuffed and round,

and the heels all crooked that look dumb with this dress, so I just sit.

Meanwhile that boy who is my cousin by first communion or something asks me to dance and I can't. Just stuff my feet under the metal folding chair stamped Precious Blood and pick on a wad of brown gum that's stuck beneath the seat. I shake my head no. My feet growing bigger and bigger.

Then Uncle Nacho is pulling and pulling my arm and it doesn't matter how new the dress Mama bought is because my feet are ugly until my uncle who is a liar says, You are the prettiest girl here, will you dance, but I believe him, and yes, we are dancing, my Uncle Nacho and me, only I don't want to at first. My feet swell big and heavy like plungers, but I drag them across the linoleum floor straight center where Uncle wants to show off the new dance we learned. And Uncle spins me, and my skinny arms bend the way he taught me, and my mother watches, and my little cousins watch, and the boy who is my cousin by first communion watches, and everyone says, wow, who are those two who dance like in the movies, until I forget that I am wearing only ordinary shoes, brown and white, the kind my mother buys each year for school.

And all I hear is the clapping when the music stops. My uncle and me bow and he walks me back in my thick shoes to my mother who is proud to be my mother. All night the boy who is a man watches me dance. He watched me dance.

*From* The House on Mango Street *by Sandra Cisneros*

71

# ELIZABETH ECKFORD
# TRIES TO GO TO SCHOOL

*When Elizabeth Eckford left for Central High School in Little Rock on a September morning in 1957, she did not know that the Governor of Arkansas had placed National Guardsmen outside the school to keep black students out. In 1954, a law had been passed to integrate schools as quickly as possible. But many Southern states ignored that law and continued to segregate students. The experience of Elizabeth Eckford and other black students prompted the Supreme Court to order the immediate desegregation of all American schools.*

I got off the bus a block from the school. I saw a large crowd of people standing across the street from the soldiers guarding Central. As I walked on, the crowd suddenly got very quiet. I walked across the street conscious of the crowd that stood there, but they moved away from me.

For a moment all I could hear was the shuffling of their feet. Then someone shouted, "Here she comes, get ready!" I moved away from the crowd on the sidewalk and into the street. If the mob came at me, I could then cross back over so the guards could protect me.

The crowd moved in closer and then began to follow me, calling me names. I still wasn't afraid. Just a little bit nervous. Then my knees started to shake all of a sudden and I wondered whether I could make it to the center entrance a block away. It was the longest block I ever walked in my whole life. Even so, I still wasn't too scared because all the time I kept thinking that the guards would protect me.

When I got right in front of the school, I went up to a guard. But he just looked straight ahead and didn't move to let me pass him. I didn't know what to do. Then I looked and saw that the path leading to the front entrance was a little further ahead. So I walked until I was right in front of the path to the front door. I stood looking at the school—it looked so big! Just then the guards let some white students go through.

The crowd was quiet. I guess they were waiting to see what was going to happen. When I was able to steady my knees, I walked up to the guard who had let the white students in. He too didn't move. When I tried to squeeze past him, he raised his bayonet and then the other guards closed in and they raised their bayonets.

They glared at me with a mean look and I was very frightened and didn't know what to do. I turned around and the crowd came toward me. They moved closer and closer. Somebody started yelling, "Lynch her! Lynch her!"

I turned back to the guards but their faces told me I wouldn't get help from them. Then I looked down the block and saw a bench at the bus stop. I thought, "If I can only get there I will be safe." I don't know why the bench seemed a safe place to me, but I started walking toward it.

When I finally got there, I don't think I could have gone another step. I sat down and the mob crowded up and began shouting all over again. Someone hollered, "Drag her over to this tree! Let's take care of the nigger."

Then a white lady came over to me on the bench. She put me on the bus and sat next to me. The next thing I remember I was standing in the front of the School for the Blind, where Mother works. I ran upstairs until I reached Mother's classroom. I wanted to tell her I was alright. But I couldn't speak. She put her arms around me and I cried.

*From* The Long Shadow of Little Rock *by Daisy Bates*

# CREW CUT

*A haircut may seem like a small thing to a grown-up, but for this boy who was growing up in the 1950s, it was very important.*

I wasn't allowed to have a crew cut. I had cowlicks instead. A crew cut would have solved the cowlick problem.

Although the crew cut belonged almost entirely to boys eleven and younger, it was a man's haircut. A crew cut was all stubble and bristle—brisk and stiff and stinging to the touch.

And I could never have one. Instead, I had to keep my part straight.

Every other Saturday, I got driven to the barbershop, where a quivering little man, so tiny he had to stand on a box, wrapped tissue paper around my throat and proceeded to straighten my part, trim my sideburns and shave the back of my neck with a seven-inch razor of shivering steel.

A single crew cut, timed to hit maybe sometime around the second week in June, would have seen any kid easily through the end of August. By that time, the cowlicks would have been back in place in plenty of time for the start of a new school year. As it stood, however, the top of my head required constant vigilance.

Every other kid I knew was part of a new, modern age, sleek and streamlined. Even my cousins from High Point, North Carolina, had crew cuts—one of them even had a brush cut; another one of them even had a burr. I, on the other hand, looked like something out of an *Our Gang* comedy.

*From "Shear Energy" by John Bridges*

74

# In the 1960s . . .

Martin Luther King, Jr., gave his "I Have a Dream" speech in 1963.

President John F. Kennedy was elected in 1960 and assassinated in 1963.

Neil Armstrong walked on the moon on July 20, 1969.

Favorite books were *Where the Wild Things Are*, *A Wrinkle in Time*, *The Cricket in Times Square*, and *Harriet the Spy*.

Popular TV shows were "Star Trek," "Batman," "Get Smart," "The Man From U.N.C.L.E.," "The Patty Duke Show," and "Gilligan's Island."

Popular dances had names like the Twist, the Mashed Potatoes, the Monkey, the Watusi, and the Frug.

Popular styles were miniskirts, boots, long straight hair (for boys and girls), tie-dyed shirts, and colorful flower prints.

Favorite toys included Slinky, Silly Putty, fashion dolls like Barbie and Tressie, G.I. Joe dolls for boys, and Colorforms.

Favorite movies were Disney's *101 Dalmatians* and *Mary Poppins*.

# POSSIBLY YOUR ASTRONAUT

*In the early 1960s, President Kennedy said that Americans would work to put a man on the moon. Ever since, children have dreamed of joining that great adventure. Some of those hopes are shared in these letters to the National Aeronautics and Space Administration.*

**Dear Mr. President,**

If you want a volunteer for the moon, Our Music Teacher will be ready to try (although she doesn't know this she has 480 kids behind her). (It's O.K. if she doesn't come back.)

P.S. Please write back if you want her.

Yours sincerely

All 480 kids

**Dear Sirs:**

I've dreamed of going to the moon for some time and I am asking to go with you. If possible I would like to come back too.

Calvin

**Dear Commanding General,**

I think it would be better to try a boy out for the Project Mercury for two reasons. First reason. He would weigh less than a man. Second reason. Boys don't panic very easily.

Possibly Your Astronaut

76

**Dear Mr. Von Braun,**

I am a girl of eleven years old and my first ambition next to going to heaven is to shake your hand.

Everyone thinks that I am a nut because I like jets and rockets. Dad says there are no women rocket scientists but I won't give up.

Sincerely yours,
Diane

**Dear Astronots,**

We are Patty, Paula, Nancy, Jean, Kathy and Eddie. I am Eddie. We would like to know something very special. It is Top Secret. But we are sworn to secretsy. We would like to have the secret fuel that makes the rocket go up. We need it badly.

Yours truly,
All of us

**Dear Dr. Von Braun,**

I know you are a busy man, but I think you will come immediately when you find out that I have the plans for a sun-powered Space Ship.

Signed
Greg

# ON KING ISLAND

*In 1963 and 1964, twelve-year-old Esther Atoolik kept a weekly logbook about her school and home. Her life was quite different from that of most children who were growing up in America at that time. She lived on King Island, off the coast of Alaska, which became our forty-ninth state in 1959.*

**October 25**

No school for three days. A big rainstorm washed away all the snow. Big rocks slid down and hit the school at one end. Teacher Roger and Adsun and Charlie had a job making the corner stand up again, so that no water came in. Lucky no windows were broken, Adsun said.

**November 22**

Teachers told us about Pilgrims and Thanksgiving. Dixon told us turkey is the best bird to eat. We told him here the best food is beluga stew. Just then Father Tomas came to tell us the sad news he heard on his radio. Our U.S. President Kennedy has been shot dead. Soon our whole village came to talk about this big news. Father Tomas said a prayer, and we felt sad for this bad happening. Marie made tea for everyone, and there was no more school this day.

**December 6**

The hunters are catching many seals. The big boys were not in school this week. They are hunters, too. Teacher Roger also. Our mothers were busy cutting up the seals. The rest of us helped them after school. Now there is much good food to eat. Much oil and good skins. Everyone is busy.

**February 7**

A big day this week. The U.S. Navy icebreaker *Burton Island* arrived. Everyone on King Island watched the big ship ram into the ice to get closer to shore. The *Burton Island* comes every year. We dress up, greet her, trade our ivory carvings for candy and cigarettes. The *Burton Island* has a doctor and dentist. Teachers lined up everybody to be examined.

We all were invited to see the big movie about cowboys. Then the men on the ship passed out cake and bananas, apples, and oranges. Everyone got some before the ship left. Big day.

**March 6**

Teachers showed slides on toothbrushing. A toothbrush danced up and down over teeth all by itself. Everyone got a new toothbrush. Everyone wanted a red one. Bits of the red handle make the best lures for bullhead fishing.

*From* Good-bye My Island *by Jean Rogers*

# MEET THE BEATLES

*When the Beatles first arrived from England, they were an instant success. Children all over the country played their records, imitated the way they dressed, and even got "Beatle" haircuts. No one had ever seen anything quite like them. But at that time no one knew that John, Paul, George, and Ringo would forever change American music.*

My sister was the first in our family to hear about the Beatles. She was three years older than me and always seemed to learn about this kind of important information first. The first time the Beatles were on TV, she persuaded our whole family to watch. It was a Sunday night in February 1964: "The Ed Sullivan Show." Every time Ed even mentioned their name, the audience—mostly teenage girls—went absolutely crazy.

Finally the Beatles came onstage and sang "I Want to Hold Your Hand." And then they shook their heads, showing off their famous long hair. The girls in the audience screamed and cried and jumped up and down. I had never seen anything like it. My sister was acting almost as crazy, shouting out each Beatle's name: John, Paul, George, and Ringo.

"You call that music?" my father asked us. He looked a bit shocked. "What a racket!" My mother liked the Beatles better. She thought Paul was the cutest. "Except for that *hair*," she added.

But for my sister and me, that first song was like a magic spell. The next day at school, everyone was talking about the Beatles. We picked our favorite and soon knew all the words to their songs. We bought Beatle posters, trading cards, lunch boxes, and T-shirts. We even imitated their British accent. A new word was invented to describe our devotion—*Beatlemania.*

# In the 1970s and 1980s . . .

The first Earth Day was celebrated on April 22, 1970.

Little League was opened to girls in 1974. Gymnastics became a new favorite sport.

Popular movies were *Ghostbusters, E.T.: the Extra-Terrestrial, Close Encounters of the Third Kind, Star Wars, Raiders of the Lost Ark,* and Disney's *The Little Mermaid.*

Popular TV shows were "Mork and Mindy," "The Brady Bunch," "Little House on the Prairie," and "Happy Days."

"Sesame Street" became the most popular children's TV show ever.

Fun fads included Frisbees, Rubik's Cubes, skateboards, Cabbage Patch Kids dolls, and video games like Space Invaders and Pac-Man.

Popular dances were the Hustle and Moonwalking.

Michael Jackson's album *Thriller* sold more than 20 million copies, making it the best-selling album ever.

Favorite children's books were *A Light in the Attic, Free to Be . . . You and Me, Doctor De Soto,* and the *Sweet Valley High* series.

# DEAR SESAME STREET

*American children were the first to learn their numbers and letters from "Sesame Street." Today, "Sesame Street" fans include children from all over the world in more than eighty countries. Here are just a few of the many letters this show receives every day.*

**Dear Oscar,**

Here's a piece of trash for you.
Nathan

**Dear Prairie Dawn,**

Whenever I see you on "Sesame Street," I notice you don't have a nose. So I made one for you! Here it is—you can smell things with it—good things like Roast Beef.

You will look pretty with this nose because I put glitter on it.

Love,
Katie

**Dear Sesame Characters,**

I have been watching your program since I was two years old. I love it. I am eight now.

Now, my three year old brother watches your show. My mom thanks you because my brother learned all of the letters from your show.

Thank you,
Your friends,
Helaina and Andrew